THE GETAWAY

MARNIE VINGE

YELLOW TRUCK MEDIA, LLC

For you, because it probably happened in your school, too

ONE

DEATH DROVE me out of this place and death brought me back.

I knew my father would die, but I didn't expect him to have a heart attack on a boardwalk Ferris wheel. He was gone before the gondola came back down to the ground. He didn't have a chance.

I also didn't expect my mother to want to bury him in California, near my childhood home. We'd all left the state after I graduated from high school, shedding horrible memories that permeated the summer after my senior year of high school. All of us had made lives elsewhere. We started fresh. Me in Chicago, my parents in New York. But California had been Dad's favorite place we'd ever lived, Mom swore. And she wanted to spread his ashes standing at the end of the same boardwalk he died above.

I'd thought it was morbid, but I was hardly one to instruct another person on how to grieve properly. After my best friend Mel died in a car accident, I'd done my fair share of weird grieving behaviors, most of them self-destructive. I'd been in the same car but had only sustained some severe injuries even though she'd hit a redwood tree in the mountains. Survivor's guilt wore me thin in the years just after the accident.

I swore when I got on the plane from Chicago that I wouldn't let any of the old feelings seep through the cracks in my mind like smoke entering a room beneath a closed door. I came here for my father's memorial and I'm leaving as soon as my mom opens this container and tosses the ashes out into the bay.

"Well?" she prompts me, turning and looking at me with watery eyes. There's something about the set of her jaw that dares me to challenge her. "Aren't you going to say something?"

I stare, transfixed by her pain. She's beautiful, my mother. And right now, she's vulnerable.

I want to tell her I was never close with Dad. That I don't know *what* to say. On the tip of my tongue is the thought that this is all ridiculous. It's macabre. He died atop the Ferris wheel just to our southeast. I glance over my shoulder at the monstrosity as it moves, half ex-pecting to see his ghost waving from the top.

But he's not there.

I turn back to my mother and look at the urn.

A whole human reduced to gravel. They gave him to us in a plastic box that contained a plastic bag that was marked with a metal tag that looked like it belonged on the D-ring of a dog collar. Instead of *Fido*, it had some random number engraved on it. Not even his name. It made me imagine him being shoved into the crematory after they swept some other poor soul out, their ashes mingling because it's impossible to get them all out of the oven.

Maybe that's why it's a number and not a name. It's not entirely Henry Grove, but mostly him. For a moment, I imagine the seal on a bottle of orange juice: *100% juice blend!*

I picture a label slapped onto the bag of gravel: *100% Henry blend!*

"Nancy!" My mom loses patience as I zone out.

"Umm—" I hesitate, struggling to find words. Something that shouldn't be hard for a journalist. "He was a good dad," I say.

"Jesus Christ, Nancy, is that the best

you've got?" she asks. Then she smiles sadly at me. "I guess I don't have anything better to say. I'd expect more from you, though." She reaches out and squeezes my hand. "Having put you through journalism school."

"Well, I never studied obituary writing." I smile back at her.

"I guess we might as well open this and do the damn thing," she says as she drops my hand. She tries to get the zip tie off the top of the bag, but it won't budge. I help her tear a hole in the plastic.

"Together?" she asks.

I nod, and the two of us shake the bag out over the bay and say goodbye to my father.

WE PART WAYS AFTERWARDS. She heads to an old friend's house. A lady she was close with as I was growing up. I go back to the hotel, not in the mood for stirring up memories. I take the most direct route, avoiding any of the places Mel and I used to frequent.

My hotel towers above the city, high and removed from the places below that hold so many of my most prized moments with Mel.

I grab a water bottle from the mini fridge, suspending any irritation I might feel about the price of it, and I walk over to the floor to ceiling windows. I catch sight of my reflection projected out into the cloudless blue sky over the city, but shift my focus further out.

I see the ocean, and I'm immediately brought back to a night with Mel, drunk on Smirnoff Ice that we bought from a gas station not known for checking IDs, stumbling down to the water with our shoes in our hands. It was near midnight and the sky was clear, just like it is now. The stars were bright and the world before us felt infinite.

The fifteen-year high school reunion

is this weekend. An unfortunate coincidence, because under any other circumstances, I wouldn't be caught dead on the west coast at such a time. I wasn't popular in high school and the idea of seeing my peers fifteen years later holds no appeal.

I had friends. Mel and I had friends. There was a group of us that ran around together. Danny, Jack, Mel, me, and our favorite English teacher, Mr. Bloodsmyth. He was an import from the UK and made a big splash with his accent during his first year at our high school. All the girls had crushes on him, me included. Bloodsmyth was probably in his early thirties when we were on the edge of eighteen. We all stayed after class with him to talk about this and that, sometimes books that he'd recommended us, sometimes life.

I wonder how he's doing.

I wonder how Danny and Jack are

doing. I haven't heard from any of them in years.

I made a conscious decision to separate myself from that summer on social media. I'm not friends with anyone from high school. My sole goal after that May was to put that weekend at Danny's dad's cabin as far behind me as possible.

I step away from the window and place my water bottle on the nightstand. My flight is this evening and I have an entire afternoon in front of me. I crawl onto the bed and grab the remote. I find a true crime show and set the alarm on my phone.

Before I know it, I drift off to sleep.

TWO

I WAKE in that dazed state that always accompanies a nap later in the day. Not immediately sure what time it is, I reach for my phone on the nightstand. I shoot up when I see the time. 7:33pm. My flight is in an hour.

I throw myself out of bed, my face hot from the nap. I shuffle into my shoes and gather my things, ready to head back to Chicago. The accelerator will be my friend on the way to the airport in the rental. I'll make it just in time.

But just as I'm throwing on my cardigan, my phone dings with a notification. The sound of email. I glance at it as I shrug my shoulders and pull my hair out of the back of the light sweater.

Flight 559 to Chicago has been canceled due to weather.

And as if on cue, thunder booms loud enough to rattle the windows and lightning strikes so close that it illuminates the entire room. I jump, startled, and drop my phone to the carpeted floor. It's only then that I notice the sound of the rain. Thunder rattles the glass again. Another lightning strike, still close. But this time, I don't jump.

I pick up my phone and touch the notification.

The airline app gives me the same information in a few more words. They have canceled the flight because a severe storm is rolling into the Bay Area.

Jesus. It must be bad if they're canceling flights.

The next available one is tomorrow

evening. I book it and sigh. With nowhere to go, all the adrenaline that dumped into my veins makes me acutely aware of everything. And that's when I notice it.

A dusty pink envelope just this side of the hotel room door, like someone slid it under.

I tuck my phone into my pocket and go over, plucking the envelope from the floor. I tear it open at the top and pull out a handwritten note. Before I read it, I flip the envelope over, sure that there's been a mistake.

But in scrawled handwriting, I see my name.

Nancy Grove

Not an accident after all, then.

I look back at the folded note and open it. Then I read.

Nancy,

Heard you were in town for your dad's memorial. I'm so sorry to hear he passed. Jack and I are going up to the Getaway this weekend in honor of the fifteen-year anniversary of everything. And of course, as a means not to have to go to the real reunion. Hope we'll see you tonight. Stay over if you'd like.

Love always,
Danny

I smile as I read his name. I'm filled with warmth. Danny is one of the few people from that time that I look back on fondly.

The Getaway. God, how long has it been since I went there?

Fifteen years, actually.

Mel and I made so many wonderful memories there. All of us. Mel, Danny, Jack, me, and Mr. Bloodsmyth. The Getaway was how Danny's father referred to the cabin. It was just across the bridge, deep into the forested mountains beyond Sausalito. Remote, but not so far that you couldn't be in town after an hour's drive.

Danny must have had the note hand-delivered after realizing I was in town.

And lucky for him, my flight's canceled.

What could it hurt?

I don't have to be at the airport until tomorrow evening. I could stay at the cabin until then.

The rain seems to let up.

The drive shouldn't be bad. I look out the window again, over the city.

Then I grab my things, and head for the lobby, ready to check out.

PUDDLES in the parking lot reflect flares of yellow from several light poles. I shove my suitcase into the backseat and then head out toward the bridge. I glance off into the night and the sea is dark, ominous. Rain mists the window, but for now, the storm is taking a break. I turn on the radio and find the classical station and drive up into the mountains.

The Getaway is near the Muir Woods, nestled into the mountainside off a twisting road. It's hidden; hence the name Danny's father gave it. We went out there all the time during our senior year. Drinking, partying, doing stuff we shouldn't. All the while I had the most ridiculous crush on Bloodsmyth, as he insisted we call him off the clock.

He was the most fun teacher I ever had. Bloodsmyth was invested in our decisions and our futures, doing more than other teachers to ensure we all got the resources we needed for our various passions. He supplied me with extra books endlessly, some from his own collection. Volumes we didn't cover in class but that he'd been sure I'd enjoy.

I'd always daydreamed about screwing up the courage to kiss him one day after school if the two of us ever found ourselves alone. But I never did it. Looking back, I'm glad I didn't make an ass out of myself and ruin the only relationship with a mentor I'd ever have.

After the accident, we lost touch. Things were never the same between any of us. I think we all wanted distance from one another. It felt like death might infect us, one by one. That Melanie had been patient zero and her accident the result of a virus. For years, I thought I must be next. That my death was imminent. It took waking up to all my self-destruction in my mid-twenties to realize death wasn't coming for me; I had to save myself.

At the edge of Sausalito, I see a gas station. I stop and head inside, intent on grabbing something for Danny. My mother taught me it was poor form to show up at a party without a gift for the host.

I settle on a bottle of white wine and pay for it, giving the cashier a smile that feels just as forced as the one she returns. I scurry out to the car and get back on the road, hoping to make it to my destination before the storm hits.

The road gets darker as I head up into the mountains. Finally, it's pitch, and my headlights are the only illumination to guide me. After several turns, I wonder how well I really remember this road. Do I know how to get there after all?

I think about one particular night when we were out at the Getaway. Bloodsmyth told us a story, gathered around the fire pit out back. He told us of Teddy Roosevelt's friendship with John Muir, the namesake of the woods nearby.

He told us the story of their adventure in Yellowstone, and how John Muir camped with the President for three nights and ultimately convinced him that the area needed federal protection.

Bloodsmyth had a way of telling a tale. He had that charisma about him. Bloodsmyth could draw you in and make you believe any old thing, sight unseen. He made our books come to life, stories from history, too.

I never would have another teacher like him.

It's something I can see clearly with hindsight. Something I took for granted then. I thought I'd meet another teacher like him at college. But they were cold, removed from their students. Nothing like Bloodsmyth. They couldn't have cared less if we lived or died on days we missed class, forget providing us with extra reading material or any form of nurturing a love for language and learning.

I thought of him often just after high school. I thought of all of them. It was still an open wound, and licking it meant tasting its edges, and conjuring them all to mind in multiple dimensions. It was hard in those days. Mel was always on my mind. She still is, but not in the same way. Now, I look back at our time to-gether and cherish those memories. They don't each drive a stake through my heart like they did at first. I've accepted that I don't have all of my memories from that night. We hit the tree hard.

After another turn on my way into the mountains, I see something that looks familiar. A sign posted on a tree near the road. NO TRESPASSING. I know that if I focus my eyes to the right-hand side of the road, in about one hundred yards, I'll see a redwood that, from the other direction, has a dent in its trunk. The tree that Mel and I crashed into. The tree that killed her.

I force myself to look only at the lines

of the road, even though I wouldn't be able to see the dent going this way. I inhale deeply as I pass, hoping that the old tale about graveyards is right: that if you breathe as you travel by, you might inhale the spirit of those stuck there.

I don't believe in ghosts, but I sometimes wonder if Mel might be stuck there. Trapped forever by a gruesome end that happened too fast for her to comprehend it. If she is a ghost, I hope she hitches a ride with me tonight. One last trip up to the Getaway.

I remember the road as I get closer, and finally, I see the turnoff. It's marked only by an open red gate. I pull into the gravel drive and wind my way to the cabin.

THREE

THE NIGHT IS STILL when I park in the driveway and get out of the car. The air is cool, bordering on cold, with the chill of fresh rainfall hanging in it. More thunder rumbles somewhere off to the west, distant, but promising to draw closer in the coming hours.

I stand there in the driveway for a moment, looking up at the cabin. The hanging lights on the patio are on, casting it in an orange glow. Inside, lights are on. I head up to the porch when the door swings open. A male figure darkens it, then steps out onto the light of the porch.

"Hey, you!" Danny shouts into the surrounding woods.

He jogs down the stairs to meet me and wraps me in a bear hug. Danny lifts me off the ground and I hug his neck more tightly than I meant to. He's here. Danny's solid. He's real.

He lets me down and beams at me while I readjust the wine bottle in my hand.

"I'm so sorry you had to come back to town under the circumstances and all," he says. "But I sure am glad I caught you before you left." His smile widens again.

"I'm glad you caught me, too," I say, finding myself beaming back at him.

"I had a messenger drop the note off at your hotel after I heard you were in town," he says.

For just a moment, it's like I'm stepping back in time. Danny's crow's feet fade away, so does the stubble. He's baby-faced, late to grow a beard, and beckoning Mel to hurry and get out of her car while she puts lip gloss on looking at herself in the rearview mirror.

In the present, he's bigger. Stronger. He has muscles now. He doesn't look like a skinny seventeen-year-old. His face looks older, too. There's a sadness around his eyes that I recognize instantly. We all have it.

"Come in," he says, and heads into the cabin. I follow him.

As I step inside, I don't know what I'm expecting, but it's not what I find.

The place looks exactly as it did fifteen years ago.

"Wow," I say.

"I know," Danny says. "I haven't made it my own yet."

"Is your dad gone?" I ask, glancing over at the orange couch where Mel would sit on his lap and I would bury my nose in a book Bloodsmyth had given me to keep. When they were wrapped up in each other, too preoccupied to notice, I would bring the pages to my face and inhale the scent of him.

"Six months ago," Danny says.

"I'm so sorry," I say.

"I'm sorry for you, too, Nancy," he says. I look over at him. "At least I knew my dad was dying. Your dad was a complete surprise, I'm sure. I imagine you appreciate your mother detailing his death in his obituary," he adds with a sad smile.

"I'm not sure it's better to know," I tell him. "At least with a surprise, you haven't been constantly worrying and wondering when it might happen."

He looks at me appreciatively but says nothing else about his father. I sit the wine down on the counter.

"So, who else is coming?" I ask.

"Just you, me, and Jack," he says. "Would you like something to drink?" He turns and heads for the kitchen and I follow.

"Sure. A beer would be great," I tell him.

Danny stoops and burrows into the fridge. When he emerges, he hands me a local brand of beer, specific to this place. A brand that Bloodsmyth brought when he'd come out here. I laugh.

"Wow," I say, taking it and examining the label. "It's been a long time since I've seen one of these."

"What? They don't have them in Chicago?" Danny teases. "By the way, how is it there?"

"Oh, it's fine," I say. "Just a place."

My words are hollow, the refrain of what might come next echoes in my ear: *a place where Mel didn't die.*

But I don't have to say it. Danny's already thinking it. His expression turns solemn for a moment and he looks beyond me, into our past. I watch his eyes, wondering what he sees there. What memory he's conjuring just now. Is it of Mel?

"How's life?" I interrupt him.

"It's good," he says with a nod. "Good. Lanie's a junior this year, but she's taking twelfth grade English at the high school," he says.

"Your daughter?" I ask.

"Oh, yeah," he says with a laugh. "God, I guess it has been a long time."

"Married, then?" I ask him. "Who's Mrs. Danny?"

"Oh, Mrs. Danny is ex-Mrs. Danny these days," he says with another laugh.

"I'm sorry to hear that," I tell him.

"I'm not," he says.

"Well, congratulations, then," I say with a smile.

"Here's to that," Danny says. He turns around and gets another beer out of the fridge and we toast to the dissolution of his marriage. He sticks the bottle of wine in the fridge.

"What about you?" Danny asks. "Is there a Mr. Nancy?"

"I'm afraid not," I tell him.

"I didn't imagine there was," he says. "You've always been so driven. I can't picture you wasting time on anyone," he adds with a smile.

I blush.

"I'll take that as a compliment," I tease.

"You should!" Danny says and lifts his glass to me once more. "You can never really know anyone anyway, I've found. No matter how hard you try."

I take a sip of my beer; the taste lingers on my tongue. It's another moment where I feel myself step through time. In the memory, I'm sitting at the fire pit out back, Bloodsmyth across from me. I look up at him and, amid everyone else's conversation, he smiles at me. It's just a moment, but my teenage heart interpreted it as far from reality as possible. I thought maybe if I was just older, we would fall in love.

The thought makes me smile. The naiveté of a teenage girl.

"There he is now," Danny says, looking past me into the driveway. For a moment, I think he means Bloodsmyth. I turn and realize he's talking about Jack, clad in a windbreaker jacket and jeans. He jogs up to the house with a bag over one shoulder and a twelve-pack in the other.

I follow Danny to the door.

He throws it wide, and immediately Jack wraps him in a hug, slapping his back loudly.

"Hey, man," Jack says, pulling away.

"Look who's here," Danny says as he steps back. Jack's eyes find me. A huge smile breaks across his face.

"Damn, Nancy," he says. "Is that you?"

"In the flesh," I smile.

Jack comes and picks me up, spinning me in a hug. My beer sloshes, getting some on both of us.

"Sorry," Jack says with a laugh.

"No worries," I tell him.

"I've got a surprise for the two of you," Jack says.

Danny arches an eyebrow.

"Oh?" he asks. "What's that?"

"You'll just have to wait and see," Jack says.

Danny and I grab another beer, and Jack gets his first. The three of us migrate to the living room. Danny sits in his dad's old recliner and it creaks as he does. Jack takes one end of the orange seventies couch and I take the other, pulling a cro- cheted blanket on the arm across my lap.

"Wasn't sure I'd ever see this again," Jack says. "I told Danny I wasn't sure you'd come," he turns to me.

"It just so happened that they can- celed my flight this evening," I tell him. "And I got Danny's note at the hotel," I toast to Danny.

"It's crazy to be back here with you guys," Danny says. "I come up with Lanie sometimes. She loves it here."

"She's coming this weekend, isn't she?" Jack asks.

"No, her mom gave me a hard time at the last minute. Something about her sister's second wedding and Lanie needing to be at the rehearsal dinner," he waves it away like he doesn't want to get into it. I don't blame him. "Jack here works at the school. He teaches history, and he's Lanie's gymnastics coach."

I nod, glad that the two of them have stayed close over the years. Also, a little envious.

"So, just us then?" Jack asks.

"Just us," Danny confirms.

"I can't wait for the surprise to show up," Jack says with a smile. He looks between the two of us and I look at Danny, who shrugs his shoulders.

I settle in on the couch and drink the rest of my beer.

FOUR

THE RAIN PICKS up around nine and I stare out the windows, watching fat droplets slide down the glass as the storm gathers momentum outside. Wind makes tree boughs dance in the darkness, their wet leaves catching the light of the moon as they sway. I stand in the hallway that faces the backyard on one side. The bathroom is just to my left, and I excused myself about ten minutes ago. Or at least I think it's been ten minutes. I feel a little tipsy.

"What are you doing back here?" Jack whispers in the darkness and I jump.

"Jesus Christ," I whisper. "I didn't hear you coming."

"Are you watching the rain?" Jack asks.

He steps up beside me. I'd forgotten just how tall he is.

He's got at least a foot on me. Taller than Danny by about six inches, he casts a long shadow across my feet as he steps forward and leans against the glass.

"I guess so," I tell him.

"I'm glad you came, Nancy," he says. "I really didn't think you would."

I wait for him to say the rest. When he doesn't, I let the silence hang between us, unwilling to be the first to say her name tonight. It's almost a challenge to them. I hope that one of them will bring her up before the end of the night. If they don't, it will feel like a betrayal.

I can't be the only one that still thinks about it.

That still thinks about Mel.

"I didn't have anywhere better to be," I say to Jack.

"Me, either," Jack says. There's a darkness to the statement that's comforting to me. The silence between us is a knowing quiet. Finally, Jack speaks again. "I know this is probably the last place you want to be. Why did you come?"

"I guess I just needed to be here one more time," I breathe in the darkness.

"I think about you a lot," Jack says, his voice equally soft.

"I think about you all a lot, too," I say.

"I think about that night," Jack goes on. "I think about Mel. I think about you getting hurt. It all just happened so fast, you know?"

"I know," I say, my voice barely above a whisper.

"One minute you guys were here, then I looked up and the two of you were gone," Jack says.

I'm silent, unsure of how to respond.

I have no memory of that night. I remember being at the party out here. I remember being with Danny, Mel, and Jack. I remember that Bloodsmyth even showed up. But things are fuzzy after that. Something that I was told by a brain trauma specialist was probably a result of the car crash.

Sometimes I feel guilty because I don't remember. If I did, maybe I could tell everyone what went wrong. What caused us to leave the party. Why Mel was driving so fast. Why we weren't even in her car.

Even now, fifteen years later, there are so many unanswered questions.

And I feel responsible for them. No matter how much other people tell me I'm not.

I look at Jack in the darkness.

In profile, he still looks like he did over a decade ago. The edges of his face are a little sharper. He turns to face me. His eyes are older.

"I'm glad you came," he says with a smile, and wraps one arm around me, pulling me to him.

"Me, too," I say.

———

WE GATHER at the table and the conversation drifts from memories to the present.

"You couldn't have gotten me to go to that thing if you offered me a million dollars," Jack says with a laugh, referring to the fifteen-year reunion.

"Me, either," Danny says. "God, I remember how shitty almost all of them were to us," he adds with a laugh.

"Do you remember Marcy Hanes?" I ask.

"Holy shit," Jack says. "I had almost *forgotten* her." He emphasizes the word like it would have been a sin.

"I remember when Mel gave her a piece of her mind," Danny says.

Jack and I are quiet. Danny goes on.

"She ripped her a new asshole down on the pier," he says with a smile. Danny's eyes are focused somewhere else. Somewhere in the past. "Marcy was giving her shit, like she always did, and Mel had enough. She dumped her drink right on top of Marcy's head. I still remember the look of utter shock on her face," Danny says.

"She never fucked with us again after that," I say, smiling now too at the memory.

"We had a lot of good times," Jack says. "The four of us."

I glance at Danny. His eyes are still somewhere far away.

And then there's a knock at the door.

I sit up straighter and look at Danny. He furrows his brow. He's not expecting another guest, either. For a moment, I think it might be Mel.

"Looks like my surprise is here," Jack says, standing from the table and finishing his beer. He places it on the table and heads for the door. Danny and I sit there, bewildered.

"Leave it to him to invite people without asking me. Jesus," Danny mutters to me with half a laugh.

I smile at Danny but strain my ears to listen to whatever Jack is saying to the visitor at the door.

"Come on in, man," Jack says. I hear his footsteps approaching the dining room.

I turn and I'm greeted with an unexpected sight.

There, standing before me, is James Bloodsmyth.

FIVE

INVOLUNTARILY, I jump from my seat and bound to him. I throw my arms around his neck and he squeezes me tight.

"Bloody hell, Nancy?" he says as he pulls away. He smiles wide, his left front tooth still chipped just slightly like it was all those years ago. I inhale the scent of him before he pulls away. Still the same as it was when I would press my nose to the open pages of the books he gave me. Something woodsy to it.

"How are you?" he says, smiling at me.

He looks so much older. Still hand-some, maybe even more so now.

"I'm good," I tell him. "How are you?"

"Fine, fine. Still teaching. Ran into Jack here at the liquor store," he reaches over and claps a hand on Jack's shoulder. "Heard you lot were getting together up here tonight." He beams over at Danny.

I follow his gaze.

Danny looks shocked. Like Blood-smyth is the last person he ever expected to see here tonight. I look between them. Bloodsmyth smiles at Danny and holds out a hand. Danny hesitates a moment and then shakes it. Bloodsmyth pulls him into a stiff embrace and slaps him on the back like Jack.

"Good to see you on unofficial busi-ness," Bloodsmyth says to Danny. He pulls away. "It's something to see the three of you out here again."

"Unofficial business?" I ask.

"Bloodsmyth here is still teaching. Lanie's one of his students," Jack says and steps past them into the kitchen. He calls back to see if our former teacher wants a beer.

"Sure, I'd love one," he says.

Danny says nothing, his expression unreadable. I'm trying to figure out what's going on in his head. Whatever he's feeling, it's apparent he's trying to hide it.

Jack comes back with a beer for Bloodsmyth.

"Come, sit down," Jack says, ushering all of us back into the dining room.

The rain comes down harder, hitting the panes of glass with force now. I glance outside and see the trees whipping back and forth in the wind.

"Looks like you got here just in time," I tell Bloodsmyth.

He looks over his shoulder.

"So I did," he says. "Hope you don't mind if I spend the night, Danny." He looks over at our host.

Danny pauses, staring at Bloodsmyth, completely still. Finally, he shakes his head, suddenly springing into animation.

"Not a problem," Danny says.

"Cards?" Jack asks.

I nod, eager to sit next to my old teacher. We slide into the seats nearest the window.

Jack heads to the living room to grab a deck of cards. Danny gets up to grab himself another beer.

"Would you get me one, too?" I ask.

Danny grunts, then turns and hands me a beer across the table. He sits down opposite me.

"Thanks," I nod at Danny and shift in my seat. The proximity to Bloodsmyth reminds me of countless days, sitting in the desk next to his in English class every afternoon of my senior year. Under the table, our legs almost touch. It's another thing here that opens the portal to the past. I feel my heart speed up, my breathing grow shallow. I still have a crush on him, I realize.

Maybe we never really outgrow those childhood crushes.

"Jack told me Lanie was up here with you this weekend," Bloodsmyth says to Danny.

"She's not," Danny says shortly. "She's with her mom."

"Oh," Bloodsmyth says, trying to make conversation with Danny. He comes up short. I try to fill the silence.

"Still teaching?" I ask him with a smile that feels too wide. I lean my head on my hand, elbow resting on the table.

"Still teaching," Bloodsmyth confirms with a smile. "I heard that you're in Chicago these days," he says.

I confirm with a nod.

"Ah, the Windy City," Bloodsmyth muses.

"It's looking pretty windy here tonight," Jack says as he shows up with a pack of cards. He takes the seat next to Danny's and shuffles them.

I look behind me once more and the storm is starting outside. Rain pelts the windows and I know the thunder and lightning are only going to get closer, the wind only stronger. I glance to my left and I feel Bloodsmyth's leg graze mine beneath the table.

Then he offers me a brief nod of acknowledgment in apology.

I just smile back at him, then realize I must look like an idiot. I look down, then back at Danny and Jack.

Jack suggests poker, and he deals the cards. I sort through mine on the first round, quickly realizing I have nothing of value. I bluff and bet two of the chips Jack brought from the living room.

Bloodsmyth bets, and a memory comes to me. His face when he's bluffing. He purses his lips just slightly. I glance at him out of the corner of my eye and turn my body slightly, trying to make it seem like I'm focused on the center of the table. I watch as his mouth twitches slightly. Not a good hand then, he sees me and raises me.

Danny and Jack pass, leaving it up to me to call Bloodsmyth. Confidently, I do.

"Well, shit," he says with a laugh and lays down three aces.

I huff, having nothing better and chuckle.

"You got me," I say. "It's yours."

Seems that Bloodsmyth might have changed his game. That I can't read him as well as I once did.

In a way it makes me sad. Yet another reminder of how things are different. For a moment during the hand, there was a part of me that thought Mel might come crashing through the door at any second, drenched in rain and carrying two over-sized bottles of Arbor Mist she scored from the gas station attendant that had a crush on her. I picture her, a wide grin on her face. Her hair clinging in stringy wet strands to her cheeks. Prouder of herself than for the A she just got on an AP history test.

"You alright?" Bloodsmyth asks me.

"Fine," I say, snapping my attention back to the present reality.

Danny shuffles the cards and I feel his eyes on me. On us.

I glance at him, and he doesn't look away.

I look back to Bloodsmyth.

"Just weird, you know, being up here this weekend," I offer with a nervous laugh.

This seems to register with Bloodsmyth for the first time.

"Oh, Christ," he says. "It's the anniversary today."

He throws an arm around me and pulls me closer to him.

"This has to be hard, especially on

you," he says softly. "I know you two were thick as thieves."

I nod and he wraps me closer to him. I savor the sensation of his body against mine. Such a strange way for the past and present to meet. Stranger still that even after all these years he has a hold on me.

Finally, he lets me go.

"How are you two holding up?" Bloodsmyth turns to Danny and Jack.

"I'm good," Jack says, ever stoic. He clears his throat, clearly uncomfortable discussing the meaning of the night and his emotions surrounding it.

"And you?" Bloodsmyth directly questions Danny.

"Same as always," Danny says evenly. "I still want to know what happened. Hit and runs are almost never solved, though."

"It wasn't a hit and run," Bloodsmyth corrects him.

"She was going over seventy-five down the mountain. Someone was chasing her. Probably nudged the car. She lost control," Danny says.

"Seems like she wanted to get out of here in a hurry," Jack adds.

Danny nods.

And the power goes out.

SIX

THERE'S a great rumbling of thunder just overhead and then lightning strikes behind us. The entire kitchen and dining room is lit in an unearthly shade of blue. I watch as Danny's pupils shrink before it, his face unchanged by fear if he feels any. There's something else there, a hardness that I don't think I'd picked up on before. Maybe it's the lighting. Maybe it's the conversation. Or maybe it's realizing that he needs to get the power back on.

"Jesus Christ," Jack says, jumping when the lightning strikes.

The room goes dark, minimal moonlight peeking through the heavy clouds overhead.

"It's alright," Danny says. "There's a generator out back."

I feel my heart rate recover, startled by the force of nature. I feel Bloodsmyth's leg touch mine beneath the table and I freeze. He doesn't move away, and neither do I.

We're frozen there for a moment. Jack gets up to help Danny. The two of us remain, saying nothing, not moving an inch.

"You know," Bloodsmyth says into the darkness. His voice breaks the silence and though he speaks softly, it sounds so much louder. "It was on a night like this that *Mary Shelley* conceived Frankenstein."

I smile in the darkness, the tension between us eased by his words. I laugh softly.

"I remember you telling me that," I

say. My voice comes out quietly, too. Like neither of us want to be caught together here in the darkness.

"You always were my favorite student, Nancy," Bloodsmyth confesses.

His leg still touches mine. I detect something else in his words. A promise. I don't dare speak, lest I break the spell.

"Glad you came tonight," he says. "I didn't know who would be here, other than Jack and Danny. Your father passed away. I'm sorry for that," he says. "I didn't think you'd be out here."

"Here I am," I say. "I can't stay away from this place, even when I promise myself I'm not in California to dredge up bad memories."

There's a bitterness to the last of my sentence. A sense of disappointment with myself. I made that promise. Despite that, I came when Danny called. It was like a summoning. Something deep within me responded to his beckoning. Something wounded and unresolved.

Something I couldn't have said *no* to in a million years.

"Closure is important," Bloodsmyth says. "Sometimes painful, always important. And not very often in life do we actually get it."

I nod in the darkness. I know he's right. It's what I just experienced out here with the death of my father. So many things left unsaid between us. A sense that we'd had time to make our relationship right, snatched away from us in death's talons.

"Still, I'm glad you're here," he says. He wraps an arm around me and gives my shoulders a squeeze. His hand lingers. The lights come back on, and Bloodsmyth quickly drops his arm from around me. He clears his throat, focusing once more on the cards in front of him.

Jack and Danny come back into the room.

We play several more hands and continue to drink into the night.

Lightning and thunder remain overhead, the storm seeming to pause right here in the woods. The wind picks up and a tree branch hits the window, broken from its tree in the storm. I jump at the sound and whip around. Jack laughs nervously.

Danny says nothing.

Just then, there's a great thundering crash out back. Something huge. Something heavy. And it sounds like it's hit the house.

The power goes out once again, and we all rush to the back door.

AN ENORMOUS TREE that I remember from youth lays across the back deck, which has collapsed beneath it at an angle. The generator is crushed beyond repair, and the four of us stand there, staring at the destruction just past the glass door.

"Jesus," Jack says with a whistle. "I can't remember a storm this bad up here."

"Me, either," I whisper.

Danny says nothing. He just stares at the damage.

"So much for the generator," he finally manages.

"Ah, it's not so bad," Bloodsmyth says. "What's a weekend in the woods without a little roughing it?"

"Sorry, man, but you wouldn't know the first thing about roughing it," Jack says with a smirk.

"Ouch," Bloodsmyth says, feigning a wound in his chest. "But you're correct. My idea of roughing it is staying in an American hotel without an air conditioner."

I smile at the joke.

Danny gathers some candles and we go back to the table for another few rounds of cards. The edges of my vision grow blurry with alcohol. Everything is a little fuzzy. Bloodsmyth's leg touches mine several times throughout the game. The laughter grows louder. The jokes more crude. We reminisce about the past. About school. About each other.

Finally, after a long while, Bloodsmyth excuses himself and heads to the restroom.

Conversation turns to family.

"How's your daughter, Danny?" I ask.

"She's doing alright," he says. "Handling the divorce well. Or at least as well as can be expected. I think she's looking forward to getting out on her own in a couple of years. I can't blame her. She's a good kid, though. Great student. Makes way better grades than I ever thought about," Danny adds with a smile. "She's been a little distant lately, though." His brow furrows.

"Teenagers can be that way," I say. I remember a time in my teens when my mother and father couldn't reach me. It wouldn't have mattered what they'd said. I was too wrapped up in my own little world. In my adventures with Mel. On the weekends here.

"She'll get past it," Jack adds sympathetically. "We all turned out alright."

Danny laughs loudly.

"Speak for yourself," he says.

I feel the urge to pee again and excuse myself from the table. Heading down the hallway to the bathroom, I feel my way along the wall. I think I've gone too far when I turn left and enter a room that doesn't have a sink. It's larger, a regular room. And I make out the shape of a person in the darkness, holding something. Moonlight peeks through the clouds and I see the side of Bloodsmyth's face. His hand is touching a yellow bag with a pink keychain attached to it.

"Didn't Mel have a bag like this?" he asks without looking up.

"She did, actually," I say, remembering the bag he's talking about. It was identical. An athletic bag in the style that was popular in the early 00s.

Interesting that Lanie would have the same style. But everything from that time period is making a resurgence. It's a strange thing to get to an age where the vintage fashion of the day is what you wore as a teenager.

"Odd coincidence," Bloodsmyth remarks.

"I thought you went to the bathroom," I say. "What are you doing in here?"

"Got lost," he says and I feel him move toward me in the darkness. Involuntarily, I take a step back.

"Me, too," I say. I turn and head out into the hallway. He follows me.

I stop and turn. The moonlight illuminates his face as the storm quiets outside. The air in the cabin grows warmer, making me aware of my skin. It flushes when his eyes travel to my mouth and back up again. It's a fleeting second, but it's enough to make my stomach jump.

I swallow, trying to find the right words.

Suddenly, I'm a teenager again. Unable to say anything to him, an adult. The power imbalance is back and I'm helpless against it.

Bloodsmyth leans in and places his hand on the side of my neck. He pulls me close and kisses me.

He tastes like that beer that you can only get here in Marin County. He tastes like the past, even though I've never tasted him until now. It's what might have been. He pushes me against the large window and kisses me deeper.

I reach for him and his hand finds the button of my jeans.

I gasp when he touches me. He fiddles with his own, dragging me into the bathroom.

They fall to his waist, and he presses himself against me.

His body works against mine, but he's not hard. He tries, grunting and positioning himself. Nothing happens. I feel shame flood my body. All this time later, and he doesn't even really want to do this. Maybe he still sees me as a kid. My heart sinks.

"What's wrong?" I ask in the darkness.

"Nothing," he snaps. "I just—I can't do this."

He lets go of me, leaving me sitting on the bathroom counter, naked from the waist down. He pulls his jeans up, buttons them, and flies out the door.

I sit there, the cold marble against my ass.

And I feel a tear run hot across my cheek.

SEVEN

I STAY THERE in the bathroom for a while. Splashing water on my face, I try to sober up. Although, the encounter with Bloodsmyth was plenty sobering.

The water is cool and I savor the feeling of air on my wet skin. It's grounding. A reassurance that this is only one night of many. I want to leave. I'm heading back down the mountain. Back to the airport, and hoping they've bumped my flight up. I'll sleep there all night if I have to.

I'm stuck in that netherworld that's

only accessible when you're drunk and you've done something terrible. Something that alters everything. I try to process it, hoping to dull the brute force I know it will pack when I'm sober.

I tried to have sex with Bloodsmyth just now.

He couldn't do it. For whatever reason. He didn't really give me an explanation and the only thing I can think is that it crossed some moral boundary for him.

Fucking Christ. Why didn't he think of that before he made me feel like shit?

I want to scream.

I leave the bathroom and grab my jacket at the door. I shrug it on. Everyone's talking in the dining room. The candles are out. The three of them discussing the state of the world like nothing just happened. I glance at Bloodsmyth but I can't make out his features. In the darkness, he's a black hole, sucking up all the matter around him as he moves.

I throw the door open and step out onto the porch.

The rain has all but stopped. A fine mist falls.

I run over to the car and get inside. The world around me still feels fuzzy. A sign that I'm not all the way sober yet. This isn't a good idea, but I can't bear the thought of spending the rest of the night under the same roof as Bloodsmyth. Not after that. I can't face him in the light of day.

"Nancy!" I hear Danny's voice from the porch. He jogs down the steps as I back up, turning the rear of the vehicle into the yard and pointing the nose toward the gravel drive that leads to the road.

I don't listen. I don't want him to talk me out of leaving.

I head for the road, but it's within moments that I realize I'm not leaving tonight.

Or in the morning, likely.

There's a huge fallen tree blocking the driveway.

I STARE AT THE TREE. It's massive. I can't even fathom how much it weighs. The thing is ancient. The kind of tree trunk that a professional will have to remove. There's no rolling it out of the way, either. It's lodged firmly between two other tree trunks, having come down at an angle across the end of the gravel drive just in front of the gate, sealing me inside this hell of my own making.

I sit there, car still in drive with nowhere to go. Danny appears at my window and I jump.

"Roll your window down!" he shouts from the other side. I do. "Where are you going?"

Shock colors his features.

"I just want to go," I say. I slur my words slightly. If I wasn't certain before, hearing myself speak leaves no doubt that I have no business driving.

"Just put it in park and come back inside," Danny says, coaxing me out of the car.

I do as he says, not seeing another way out. I glance up toward the house and see Bloodsmyth and Jack standing on the porch, both of them watching me. Probably wondering if I've lost my mind. At least Jack is.

Bloodsmyth knows why I left.

How fucking awkward.

Jesus, maybe we're all too drunk to have good judgment.

Danny tucks me under his coat, and we head back up to the house. The air is colder than it was when I drove out. It smells like fresh rain. Distant thunder rumbles over the mountains.

"Well, we're stuck here," Danny says as he ushers me back into the house.

I catch Bloodsmyth's eye. His face is expressionless.

They follow us inside and I go sit on the couch, hoping they won't follow me, but they all do.

"Hey, Jack," Bloodsmyth says. "Why don't you and I see if we can't salvage that generator. What do you say?" He claps a hand on Jack's shoulder in a paternal way that I know Jack won't refuse. He follows our old teacher right out the back door where they gingerly step around the hole in the deck left by the tree.

"You okay?" Danny asks me.

"I'm fine," I assure him. Even to me I don't sound alright.

"What's up? Why did you leave?" Danny asks. "It's hard being here, isn't it?" he asks. "I shouldn't have asked you to come out here."

"No, it's fine, Danny," I tell him. "It's not that."

"What happened, Nancy?" Danny asks. His tone is suddenly serious.

"I just—I'm an idiot, that's all," I tell him. "We've all had too much to drink."

"What happened?" he presses, reaching out a hand for my wrist now.

"I almost had sex with Bloodsmyth," I tell him with a rush of shame. It sounds even worse when I speak it aloud. How absurd. We haven't seen each other in fifteen years, and now, on the anniversary of my best friend's death I'm going to act out some teenage dream?

Jesus Christ, Nancy.

"Are you serious?" Danny asks.

"Dead," I say, annoyed with myself. Even more annoyed that I caved and told Danny.

"Mel said something to me that night when she rushed out of here with you," Danny says.

"What? She did?" I sit up straighter. It's like he's telling a ghost story. The hair on the back of my neck stands on end. This is new information. Danny's never told me this.

"Yeah, it was gibberish to me then," he admits. "She said *he* was going to hurt you. Didn't say who. Said she needed to get you out of here before *he* did the same thing to you."

"What?" I ask.

"It meant nothing to me then," Danny says. "So I told no one. I thought she was hysterical. High or something. Paranoid. She used to get paranoid when she smoked weed," he says. I remember that about her. It's something I hadn't thought about in ages. "She came running up to me, asking where her keys were. I told her I didn't know. That if she'd dropped them in the bowl, they were still in there. But she couldn't find them. She freaked out, and I gave her the keys to the restored Mustang," he says. "And then you guys were gone."

"Who do you think she was talking about?" I ask.

"I asked around for years. If anyone ever saw anything that night. No one ever came forward with anything. If they had seen anything, they weren't letting on. I ran into the old art teacher, Mrs. Silvers, a couple years ago. And she had some thoughts about the whole thing. She asked me if any of that was ever resolved. She was older then. I was afraid she might have been senile with the things she said."

"What did she say?"

"Said that what happened that weekend wasn't an accident," he says. He looks at me in the darkness and I see moonlight glint off his eyes.

"How was it not an accident?" I ask.

"Silvers said there was an investigation that year. Into one of the teachers," Danny goes on.

I stare at him in the darkness.

"Bloodsmyth," he says.

"Oh, my God," I whisper. "Did nothing come of it?" I ask.

"Nothing," Danny says. "No one ever confirmed anything."

"So, he didn't do anything?" I ask, a sinking feeling in my gut. I think about the way he was in the bathroom. Him struggling to get hard. Me thinking it had to do with the fact that he still saw me as a kid.

Maybe it was that I *wasn't* a kid anymore.

"I didn't say that," Danny says. "No one proved anything. But I remember the look in Mel's eyes that night. She dragged you out of here. And right after the two of you left, Bloodsmyth was out the door."

"Jesus," I whisper, shaking the previous thought. "You don't really think he could do anything like that, do you?" I ask.

"I think people can surprise you," Danny says.

EIGHT

JACK AND BLOODSMYTH come back into the cabin, the generator still just as crushed as it was when they went outside. I'm sure that Bloodsmyth knew they couldn't fix it. He just wanted a reason not to have to look me in the eye.

As they walk in, I grab the glass of water I'm drinking and head to the kitchen, excusing myself. I look at Bloodsmyth and his eyes meet mine for a moment. I try to read them. Try to see what I can interpret after all these years. But they're dark. Almost black and unread-

able. Like he's put up some sort of bar-
rier. The warmth I've always known
them to hold is gone. And for the briefest
moment, I recognize something in them.

It sends a shiver up my arms. I tuck
them against my sweater and go refill my
glass.

I hear the guys talking in the living
room. The *men*. Hard to think of them
that way, I realize. The last time we were
all here together we were fifteen years
younger.

A memory comes to me. Mel trying to
drag me out of Bloodsmyth's classroom
that May. I wanted to linger, talk to him
about something. He had asked me to
stay. Mel begged me to go with her. She
told me she couldn't be late to math
again. I told her he'd write us a pass, but
she didn't want it. She got angry and left
me behind.

Bloodsmyth left a story in my cubby-
hole that Friday. I went to check for
homework and there were extra pages. A

copy of a story from a book. *Raping Her* had been the title. I'd thought nothing of it then. The party at the Getaway was the next weekend.

I wonder what Mrs. Silvers would say about that. If she ever had suspicions about Bloodsmyth.

I take my glass and head back into the living room. It's well past midnight and I yawn.

"I think I'm ready to call it a night," I tell Danny.

"You can have Lanie's room, Nancy," he tells me. "Jack will take the couch. And you can have the guest room," he tells Bloodsmyth.

Danny walks me down the hall to the bedroom that belongs to Lanie when she's here. I shut the door behind me. Moonlight illuminates the space. The sky is clear, though the damage to the surrounding forest is done. I spot the backpack that looks so much like Mel's. I pull it up onto the bed with me and unzip it.

I look at the tag, and a chill runs down my spine.

In faint letters, I see Mel's name inscribed next to the brand label. She had the bag with her that weekend. Had Danny kept it?

It's full of school books and binders. And then I see a loose piece of paper that looks a little worse for the wear, dog-eared on the corner and wrinkled in the middle. It's a photocopy of a page from a textbook.

I pull it out and look at it in the moonlight.

I recognize it instantly.

Raping Her: a Love Story

I hadn't understood it when he'd given it to me all those years ago. Now, it seems all too clear.

My heart thunders in my chest and I sit still on the bed, waiting until everyone goes to sleep.

WHEN THE HOUSE IS SILENT, I creep out of Lanie's room. I pad down the hall, barefoot, hoping that I'm not making too much noise as I go. Blood-smyth snores loudly in the guest room and Jack does the same on the couch as I pass them. I scurry on to the master bed-room and rap lightly on the door. I don't wait for the all clear and sneak inside.

"Danny," I hiss into the darkness.

"Nancy?" His voice is alert, like he hasn't been sleeping either.

"I found something," I say, breathless.

Danny grabs his phone from the nightstand and turns on the flashlight.

"Sit," he says and I join him on the bed. I hold out the papers, photocopied and stapled together.

"I know this story," I tell him. "I found it in Lanie's bag."

"What?" Danny asks.

"Is that Mel's bag, Danny? Did you keep it?" I ask.

He shifts uncomfortably.

"Yeah, I did," he admits. "She left it here that night. Lanie found it recently and asked if she could use it. But you went through it?"

"I just had a feeling," I tell him. It's not the whole truth. I had a feeling the bag was Mel's, not that there was something in it worth looking at. "Read it."

"*Raping Her: a Love Story*... What the hell is this? You found this in Lanie's bag?" he asks.

"Bloodsmyth left the same story for me in my cubby senior year," I tell him. "Remember those stupid cubbies? He'd put our assignments in them?"

"Yeah," Danny says. "He left you *this* story?"

"Yeah," I say. "He put a note on it. That he would see me at the cabin that weekend."

Danny is silent.

"This can't..." he mutters. "Lanie isn't..."

"He's her English teacher, isn't he?" I ask.

"Earlier," Danny says softly. "He seemed disappointed that she wasn't here."

Even in shadow, I see the rage on Danny's face.

"Slow down," I tell him.

But he stands, the papers falling to the floor.

"I'll kill him," Danny says.

"Stop, Danny," I tell him.

"No, Nancy. You don't get it. You never had kids," he says. "That night, Bloodsmyth was after the two of you. She said she needed to get you out of there before he did the same thing to you that he'd done to her."

"Did she say his name?" I ask.

Danny's jaw sets.

"I saw how he followed the two of you," Danny says. "He was the one who called in the wreck, Nancy. How can you not see this? Are you really still so in love with him you'd look past him being a *pedophile*?"

I feel like Danny's slapped me.

He's right.

All the evidence is there.

I sigh.

"What are we going to do?" I ask him.

"I don't know," Danny says. Then he gets quiet.

The kind of quiet you need to plan a murder.

NINE

IT'S THEN that the two of us hear someone shuffling around in the house.

"Come on," Danny says. I follow him.

We exit the bedroom and we find Jack in the kitchen, down on his hands and knees, searching for something.

"What's up, man?" Danny asks, his tone exasperated. He was clearly expecting a confrontation with Bloodsmyth.

"Thought I dropped something," Jack mutters, then gets back on his feet. "Why are you two up?"

"Couldn't sleep," I offer. "I wanted some company and you and Bloodsmyth were out cold," I tell him.

Jack shrugs in the moonlight and grabs a beer from the fridge.

"Still pretty cold," he tells us. "You want one?"

Danny shakes his head, and I do the same.

I'm not sure a beer would be wise. I'm going to need all five senses fully engaged for whatever comes next. Danny can't kill Bloodsmyth. But how the hell am I supposed to prevent that? Jack will stop me if he finds out what's going on. Danny will beat Bloodsmyth to death. I can see it all unfolding now. Lanie needs her dad, regardless of what happens next to Bloodsmyth.

My mind whirls.

"You okay?" Jack asks me.

"Fine," I say, almost jumping out of my skin. It's then that I realize Danny has left the room. I dart into the dark living room and find him there. I sigh with relief.

I sit down on the couch beside Danny in the living room.

"What now?" I ask under my breath.

"We wait," Danny says, rocking himself slightly back and forth. "We wait."

DAWN BREAKS and Jack sits across from us, drinking yet another beer and somehow seeming to remain sober. He's such a big guy I wonder how many, and how quickly, it would take for him to get drunk these days.

The room lightens; the darkness washed away by the early morning light. And that's when I hear Bloodsmyth stir in the guest room. My spine straightens, my muscles tighten. I don't know what's about to happen.

"Why don't we step outside?" I ask

Danny. I grab his arm and pull him upward.

He looks at me like it's the last thing he wants to do, but he comes with me.

I take him to the back patio, sliding the glass back behind us. The two of us step gingerly around the half of the deck that's collapsed under the tree. I lean against the railing, thinking that I need a moment to myself. I need to call the cops to come out here before anything truly bad happens. But I don't want to leave Danny alone.

I turn around to look at Danny, but as I do, I catch sight of Bloodsmyth walking across the living room to the kitchen.

Danny looks out over the back of the property.

Just then, I see something sticking out of the hole left by the collapsed deck. A shiny silver button against dark brown leather. I take a few steps forward and stoop, picking it up.

I open it and there's a picture of a young girl.

"I'm going inside," Danny says, and he heads back inside. He stops short when he sees what's in my hand. "Where did you find that?" His voice is cold, mechanical.

"Just here," I point to the hole.

He rushes past me.

"I'm going to fucking kill you," Danny bellows at Bloodsmyth.

Bloodsmyth looks like someone has dunked him in ice water when Danny throws the first punch and lands it across his jaw.

I turn, looking for Jack, but I don't see him. I flip the picture over in the wallet. On the back in a childish scrawl is Lanie's name with a heart.

Jesus Christ.

"Her picture's in your wallet!" Danny yells at Bloodsmyth.

Bloodsmyth tries to stop the next punch, but he's too slow. Danny breaks his nose and blood spurts across the white wall of the living room.

I dial 911 and speak fast into the receiver. I tell them what's going on and the dispatcher speaks back.

"We'll get someone out there," she says. "Crews are working on the trees on the road out there. Don't get in the middle of it," she instructs. I hang up, not feeling like I have much of a choice.

Jack runs back into the room, shocked at the turn of events.

Bloodsmyth is down on the floor and Danny kneels over him, landing one punch after another.

I flip the photo again, and I see the driver's license.

"Danny!" I shout.

Danny doesn't hear me. He's beating Bloodsmyth to death. I hear another crunch of bone beneath Danny's fists. I run to his back and I pull him by the shoulders. He reaches back and hits me with an elbow. I go flying backwards. The wallet tumbles to the floor. I grab it, looking at it again to make sure I'm not wrong.

"Danny!" I shout. *"Danny! It's not his wallet!"*

Danny slows his punches. I repeat myself and run to him, pushing him off of Bloodsmyth. I reach around him, digging into his back pocket and pull a wallet out.

I hold them both up and open them in Danny's face.

In one wallet, is Bloodsmyth's ID.

In the other is the picture of Lanie. And Jack's ID.

Danny is silent.

He looks up at Jack.

"Wait, man," Jack says, holding up his hands.

"Jack," Danny says. "Why is my daughter's picture in your wallet?"

"She—she's my favorite kid, man," Jack stammers. "She's the star on the team, you know?" he adds with a smile.

"What about that night?" Danny

asks, looking at me. Disbelief is in his voice. "What about the poem? *He* gave her the poem."

"I--" I murmur, a memory coming to me.

It's clear as day, the night of the party. Jack, taking my drink. He disappeared for a moment. Then he came back. A few minutes later, Mel grabbed my hand and jerked me to my feet. We left then. We left because of Jack.

"What poem?" Bloodsmyth asks, hoisting himself to his elbows.

"The poem you left for me," I tell him. "About the rape," I say. "You left it in my cubby. You wrote on the back that you wanted me to come to the cabin that weekend," I say.

"I never did that," Bloodsmyth says with labored breath. He swipes at the blood on his sweater.

"I did," Jack says cooly.

We all turn to him.

"I'm the one who left it there for you,

Nancy. It's always been one of my favorites and I thought you'd get that. You loved English so much. Mel did, too. I gave it to her, too. But it scared her, and she didn't want to be around me after that. Even when I kissed her at Borders one night, she still didn't get it."

I stare at Jack in disbelief.

"Lanie's like you were. Special. She gets it," he says. "But Lanie knows that I'm a good guy. You could never see that, Nancy," he says.

I feel a coldness wash over me.

I swallow.

Jack takes a step forward.

"So, yeah, Danny. I have her picture in my wallet. And you know what? She *gave* it to me. She thought she'd be out here this weekend. I was hoping I'd get to see her," he adds with venom.

Danny looks like someone has kicked him in the stomach.

I think about Mel. About how scared she was to stay in Bloodsmyth's classroom that day. About the fact that Jack was there, too.

I think about how fast she got me out of that party.

How, if she was here, I knew exactly what she'd do.

I reach behind me.

Jack steps forward. He kicks Blood-smyth in the ribs.

"They always thought you were the creep on campus," he laughs. "I started the rumors about you that year," Jack says. "You never really knew where to draw the professional boundary."

He walks forward toward Danny.

"And you," he says. "How could you *not know*?" Jack asks with a laugh. He reaches into his back pocket and pulls out a switchblade. "Thanks for finding my wallet, Nancy," he says, holding out a hand to me. "I'll be needing that now."

Danny lunges for Jack's waist. He barrels him into the couch and Jack brings the knife down in Danny's back. He cries out.

My vision tunnels as the fire poker arcs through the air and I'm not prepared for the wet crunching sound it makes when it connects with Jack's skull.

TEN

I HEAR the sirens before I even let go of the poker.

Jack's body goes limp beneath Danny.

Danny falls to the floor on his side. I rush to him. Bloodsmyth tries to move, but he can't. He falls back to the floor, covered in his own blood.

"It's okay," I tell Danny.

His breath is shallow but I think he's going to be okay.

They have to stop in the road and climb over the fallen tree in the drive, but the EMTs are in the house faster than I expected. They rush us all to the hospital. The police question us there.

Jack doesn't make it.

After they're done, I go to check on Danny.

I hover in the doorway. He's fast asleep, a bandage around his middle.

I hear a voice from behind me.

"How are you doing?" Bloodsmyth asks.

I turn, surprised to see him. He walks up with all manner of bandages on his face and a sling on his arm.

"I'm fine," I tell him. "Are you okay?" he asks.

"Fine," he says. The two of us struggle for something to say. "I'll leave you to it, then," Bloodsmyth says. As he turns, he drops his wallet on the ground. I stoop to pick it up for him.

When I do, a picture falls out.

A young girl. About Lanie's age. About my age when I had him.

I turn it over. It's signed with *xoxo*.

I stand up and make eye contact with him. A chill runs down my arm.

"Just my niece," he blurts. He takes the wallet from my hand and limps down the hall.

ACKNOWLEDGMENTS

I need to thank my family for putting up with me as I've been prepping this novella and the following novel, *Swingers*, for publication. I've been a crazy person, and you (and the dogs) have loved me anyway.

Thank you to my editor, Collette Carmon, who always keeps me on track and makes sure I'm doing my best.

Thank you to the Psychological Thriller Readers group on Facebook and all of you who signed up for updates about *Swingers*. *The Getaway* is a little surprise to go with it!

Thank you to my writing buddies, Katie and Johnetta. We keep each other sane and out of jail.

ABOUT THE AUTHOR

I started writing when I was 7. The book was called *It Came Floating Up*. It was inspired by many trips to the beach and watching a few too many episodes of *The X-Files* with my grandmother. The book was about a monster lurking in the sargasso seaweed just off the coast of Corpus Christi. In the dedication, I wrote:

To my family, who has been there through everything.

I was 7. If only I'd known then what exactly *everything* would entail.

Since then, I've only gotten more dramatic and more obsessed with *The X-Files* and storytelling.

My books all have one thing in common: they are inspired by some element of truth either in my own life or something I pick out of a headline or a history book. Mostly, though, my writing is inspired by my own experiences and emotions, just blown up on a grander scale with a murder or two to make it exciting.

Just call me the Taylor Swift of psychological thrillers.

JOIN MY NEWSLETTER

Sign up now and get a free horror novella, The Body Snatchers. You'll also get updates, freebies, news about me and my dogs, plus book discounts and sales!

Sign up here:
https://BookHip.com/PZGBMZT

ALSO BY MARNIE VINGE

SHOP NOW

www.marniewritesthrillers.com

Psychological Thrillers

The Getaway

Swingers

For Rosie

I Remember Everything

Cold Blood

Women's Thrillers

The Way It Ends

What We Did That Night

Manspreader

The Blair Graves Files

The Haunting of Solomon House

The Holloway Hoax

The Vampire's Game

One Night in September

Short Horror Collections

Thicker Than Water

In Sheep's Clothing

The Reunion

Romance

Gunshy

www.ingramcontent.com/pod-product-compliance
Lightning Source LLC
Chambersburg PA
CBHW021932170626
46807CB00007B/3076

*9 7 9 8 9 8 8 0 9 1 8 1 3 *